# It's Your Turn, Roger!

1 3 5 7 9 10 8 6 4 2

First published in the United Kingdom 1985
by The Bodley Head Children's Books

First published in Mini Treasures edition 1998
by Red Fox
Random House, 20 Vauxhall Bridge Road,
London, SW1V 2SA

Random House Australia (Pty) Ltd
20 Alfred Street, Milsons Point, Sydney,
New South Wales 2061, Australia

Random House New Zealand Limited
18 Poland Road, Glenfield,
Auckland 10, New Zealand

Random House South Africa
PO Box 2263, Rosebank 2121, South Africa

RANDOM HOUSE UK Limited Reg No. 954009

A CIP catalogue record for this book
is available from the British library.

ISBN 0 099 26352 1

Printed in Singapore

# It's Your Turn, Roger!

## Susanna Gretz

**Mini Treasures**

RED FOX

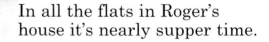

In all the flats in Roger's
house it's nearly supper time.

Roger, it's your turn
to set the table.

That's his sister calling.

I see you, Roger!

That's his little brother.

Roger, you know we all
take turns at helping.

That's Roger's dad.

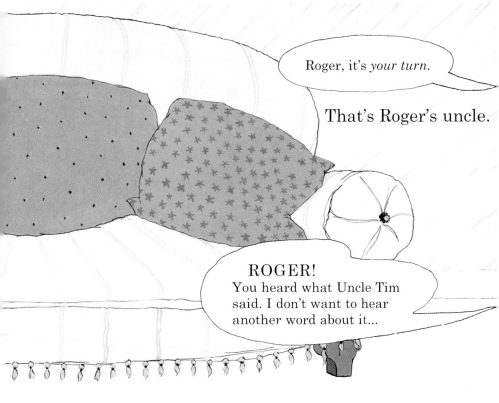

...and that's final!

That's Roger's mum.

"OK, OK," moans Roger.

"In other families you don't have to help,"
Roger grumbles.

"Are you sure?" asks Uncle Tim.
"Why don't you go and see?"

"All right, I *will*,"
says Roger.

He stomps out
of the door...

...and on upstairs.

"Come in, come in," says the family on the first floor.

"Do I have to set the table?" asks Roger.

"Certainly not, you're a guest. Come in and have some fishmeal soup."

What a fancy supper table,
thinks Roger...

...but what *horrible* soup!
"Excuse me," says Roger, and he hops upstairs.

"Come in, come in," says the family on the second floor.

"Do I have to set the table?" asks Roger.

"Certainly not, you're a guest. Come in and have some mud pancakes."

What a messy table, thinks Roger ... and
what *dreadful* pancakes!

No one notices as he slips out.

"Come in, come in," says the family on the third floor.

"Do I have to set the table?" asks Roger.

"Certainly not, you're a guest. Come in and have a little snack."

This family doesn't even *have* a table...

Roots and snails - YUK!
Roger hurries away.

"Come in, come in," says the family in the top flat.

"Do I have to set the table?" asks Roger.

"Certainly not, you're a guest. Come in and have some milky mush."

"Well..." says Roger. He *is* getting hungry.

Everyone in the top flat is busy getting the supper table ready.

Roger sits by himself
and watches.
    If I weren't a "guest",
I could help too, he thinks.

Supper time

"What's a guest?" he asks someone.
"Well... guests don't really live here."
"Oh," says Roger. "Now where *I* live..."

Just then a special smell creeps
all the way upstairs to the top flat.

"Where *I* live," shouts Roger,
"there's something *good* for supper –"

"– and it's my turn to help!"

"I took your turn for you,"
says Uncle Tim.
"I'll take your turn tomorrow,"
says Roger, between mouthfuls.

Worm pie for dessert - whoopee! Roger's favourite.